P9-CSW-033

WELCOME TO
PASSPORT TO READING
A beginning reader's ticket to a brand-new world!

Every book in this program is designed to build read-along and read-alone skills, level by level, through engaging and enriching stories. As the reader turns each page, he or she will become more confident with new vocabulary, sight words, and comprehension.

These PASSPORT TO READING levels will help you choose the perfect book for every reader.

READING TOGETHER
Read short words in simple sentence structures together to begin a reader's journey.

READING OUT LOUD
Encourage developing readers to sound out words in more complex stories with simple vocabulary.

READING INDEPENDENTLY
Newly independent readers gain confidence reading more complex sentences with higher word counts.

READY TO READ MORE
Readers prepare for chapter books with fewer illustrations and longer paragraphs.

This book features sight words from the educator-supported Dolch Sight Words List. This encourages the reader to recognize commonly used vocabulary words, increasing reading speed and fluency.

For more information, please visit passporttoreadingbooks.com.

Enjoy the journey!

Little, Brown and Company

Hachette Book Group
1290 Avenue of the Americas, New York, NY 10104
Visit us at lb-kids.com

Little, Brown and Company is a division of Hachette Book Group, Inc.
The Little, Brown name and logo are trademarks of Hachette Book Group, Inc.

The publisher is not responsible for websites (or their content) that are not owned by the publisher.

First Edition: April 2015

Library of Congress Control Number: 2014956315

ISBN 978-0-316-25640-7

10 9 8 7 6 5 4

CW

PRINTED IN THE UNITED STATES OF AMERICA

Passport to Reading titles are leveled by independent reviewers applying the standards developed by Irene Fountas and Gay Su Pinnell in *Matching Books to Readers: Using Leveled Books in Guided Reading*, Heinemann, 1999.

MARVEL

AVENGERS
AGE OF ULTRON

Hulk to the Rescue

By Adam Davis

Illustrated by **Ron Lim, Andy Smith,** and **Andy Troy**

Based on the Screenplay by **Joss Whedon**

Produced by **Kevin Feige, p.g.a.**

Directed by **Joss Whedon**

LITTLE, BROWN AND COMPANY
New York   Boston

Attention, Avengers fans!
Look for these words
when you read this book.
Can you spot them all?

robot

metal

army

hammer

The Avengers are on a mission.

They must defeat an evil robot
named Ultron.
He wants to take over the world.

Ultron wants a special metal. It will make him so strong that the Avengers can not stop him!

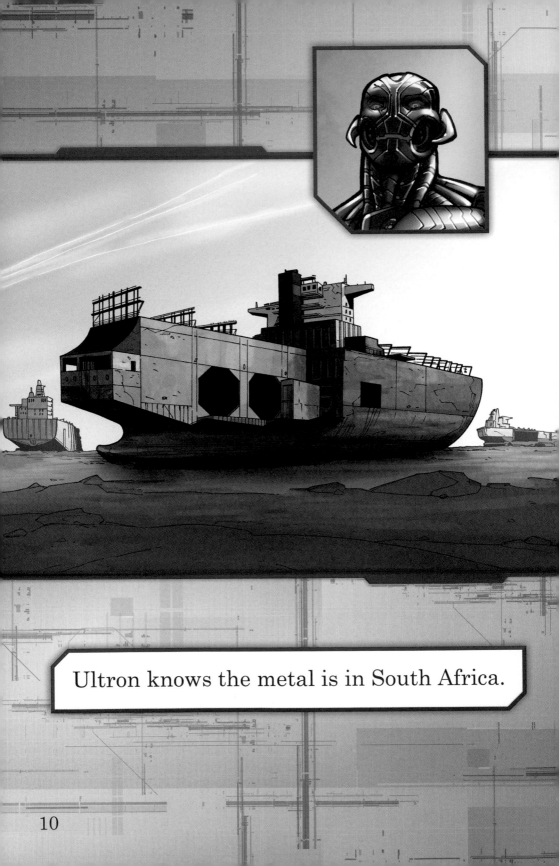

Ultron knows the metal is in South Africa.

He can get it from a man named Klaue. Klaue sells bad things to bad people.

The Avengers arrive to stop Ultron.

This fight should be easy.

It is only Ultron against all the Avengers!

Hawkeye watches everything
from up high.
He sees an army of Ultron's Sentries!

The robots look just like Ultron.
This fight will not be easy after all!

Iron Man, Thor, Captain America, Black Widow, and Hawkeye battle the Sentries.

Hawkeye fires arrows at the robots.
He stops them with perfect shots!

Black Widow and Thor fight Ultron.

Widow uses her Widow's Bites.

Thor uses his mighty fists and hammer.

Ultron is tough.

The blows do not damage his metal body!

Then, Ultron gets even more help! Pietro and Wanda rush into the battle. The brother and sister are mad at the Avengers.

Pietro runs very, very fast.

He knocks down the Super Heroes!

Wanda has powers, too.
She uses strange energy to hurt
the Avengers' minds.
Thor, Black Widow, and
Captain America cannot stop her.
She is too strong.

It is up to Iron Man to beat Ultron now.

His friends are hurt!

He tries to stop Ultron from getting away.

Ultron is too powerful.

Even Iron Man's armor cannot hurt his metal body.

It looks like the Avengers are losing!

But the heroes have a secret weapon.
He is the Hulk!

The Hulk jumps into the air
and lands on Ultron's Sentries.
The robots are crushed!

The Avengers beat Ultron and his Sentries.
Then they stop Pietro and Wanda.

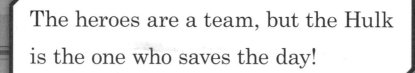

The heroes are a team, but the Hulk is the one who saves the day!